This edition published by Parragon in 2013
Parragon
Chartist House
15–17 Trim Street
Bath BA1 1HA, UK
www.parragon.com

ISBN 978-1-78186-645-0

Printed in China

Aladdin

Bath • New York • Singapore • Hong Kong • Cologne • Delhi
Melbourne • Amsterdam • Johannesburg • Shenzhen

In the Arabian desert, an evil sorcerer named Jafar told a thief named Gazeem to enter the Cave of Wonders to get a magic lamp. As Gazeem walked toward the cave, a voice boomed: "Only one may enter here, one whose worth is far within—the Diamond in the Rough!"

The cave wouldn't let Gazeem inside.

"I must find this . . . Diamond in the Rough," said Jafar.

The next evening, in the city of Agrabah, a poor young man named Aladdin and his monkey, Abu, sat down to eat their first meal in days. But Aladdin realized that there were others worse off than them, and he gave the bread to some hungry children.

"Someday, Abu, things are going to change," Aladdin said as he stared out at the Sultan's palace.

Meanwhile, in the palace, Princess Jasmine was very unhappy. Her father, the Sultan, wanted her to marry a prince—in three days' time!

"It's the law," he said. "You're a princess."

"Then maybe I don't want to be a princess anymore," she replied as she patted her pet tiger, Rajah. "If I do marry, I want it to be for love."

The Sultan was at his wit's end! He called upon his most trusted advisor—Jafar—for help.

"Jafar, I am in desperate need of your wisdom," the Sultan pleaded. "Jasmine refuses to choose a husband."

"Perhaps I can devise a solution," Jafar said. "But it would require the use of the mystic blue diamond . . ."

Jafar hypnotized the Sultan with his snake staff, then took his mystic ring. Jafar had a plan—he would persuade Jasmine to marry him. Then he would become Sultan!

That night, Jasmine decided to run away. "I can't stay here and have my life lived for me," she told Rajah. "I'll miss you."

Outside the palace wall, Jasmine suddenly found herself alone in a new world—Agrabah's busy market.

Before long, Jasmine saw a hungry child. She took an apple from a fruit stand and gave it to him.

"You'd better be able to pay for that!" bellowed the huge fruit seller. The princess hadn't realized she would have to pay. Luckily, clever Aladdin helped her get away.

"So, where are you from?" Aladdin asked.

"I ran away," Jasmine answered with a sigh. "My father is forcing me to get married."

By now, Jafar had discovered that Aladdin was the only one who could enter the Cave of Wonders! He ordered the Sultan's guards to bring Aladdin to the palace.

Jasmine tried to save Aladdin by revealing that she was the princess, but the guards didn't listen.

Locked away in a dungeon, Aladdin could think only of the beautiful princess he would never see again.

Then, suddenly, an old prisoner stepped out from the shadows. "There is a cave filled with treasure," he said. "Treasure enough to impress your princess."

Aladdin followed the old prisoner through a secret passage and out into the desert. Soon, he and Abu were standing before the Cave of Wonders.

A booming voice told Aladdin that he could go inside, but told him not to touch any treasure—only the lamp.

"Fetch me the lamp and you shall have your reward," the old prisoner promised.

But as Aladdin reached for the lamp, Abu touched a gem. The voice of the cave spoke: "You touched the forbidden treasure! You shall never see the light of day again!"

Aladdin and Abu raced for the entrance. But as soon as the old prisoner had the lamp, he pushed Aladdin and Abu down into the collapsing cave!

"It's mine!" the old man shrieked, pulling off his disguise to reveal that he was Jafar! But when he reached into his robe for the lamp, it was gone!

A Magic Carpet appeared and caught Aladdin and Abu. It safely set them on the floor of the cave.

"We're trapped!" Aladdin cried. But then Abu held out his paw. "The lamp!" Aladdin exclaimed. The monkey had snatched it back.

Aladdin rubbed the lamp to clean off some of the dust, and the lamp began to glow. Then a cloud of smoke poured from the spout—and turned into a giant blue genie!

The Genie explained that he could grant Aladdin three wishes. Aladdin couldn't believe it!

Aladdin didn't want to waste a wish, so he tricked the Genie into getting them out of the cave.

"What is it you want most?" the Genie asked later, offering Aladdin the first of his three wishes.

"Can you make me a prince?" Aladdin asked. He wanted to impress Princess Jasmine.

"Hang on to your turban, kid!" the Genie shouted. "We're gonna make you a star!"

Dressed in royal robes, Aladdin went to the palace to speak to Jasmine's father.

"Your Majesty, I have journeyed from afar to seek your daughter's hand in marriage," Aladdin announced.

The Sultan was thrilled! But Jasmine thought Aladdin was just another snooty prince.

To try to win
Jasmine's heart,
Aladdin sneaked
up to her balcony
on the Magic
Carpet. "Please
give me a chance,"
Aladdin asked. Then he
invited her on a magical ride.

Jasmine realized that this prince was really the young man she had met in the marketplace. She thought he must have been in disguise, too.

By the end of the night, they had fallen in love!

Before long, Jafar heard
that Prince Ali and Jasmine
were growing close.

Jafar knew he had to get rid
of the prince. He ordered his
guards to chain Prince Ali up
and throw him into the sea.

Luckily, the Genie was nearby, and Aladdin used his second wish to save himself.

"Don't scare me like that, kid," the Genie said as he unchained his master.

Aladdin raced to the palace and arrived just as the hypnotized Sultan was about to order Jasmine to marry Jafar!

"Your Highness, Jafar has been controlling you with this!" Aladdin cried as he smashed the snake staff.

"Traitor!" the Sultan cried. But before the guards could arrest Jafar, the villain escaped.

Later, hiding in his laboratory, Jafar realized that Prince Ali was nothing more than Aladdin, and that he must have the magic lamp!

At dawn the next morning, Jafar's parrot, Iago, sneaked into Aladdin's room and stole the lamp.

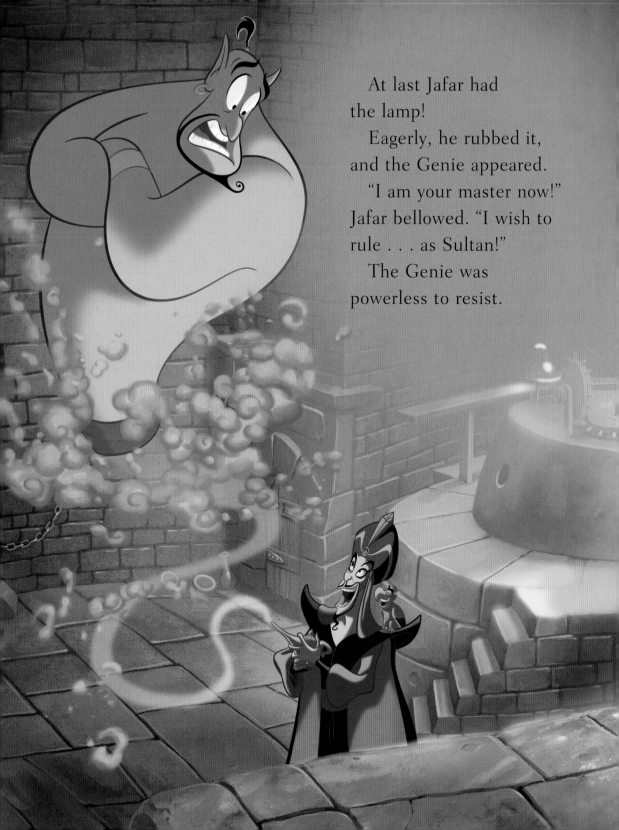

At last Jafar had
the lamp!

Eagerly, he rubbed it,
and the Genie appeared.

"I am your master now!"
Jafar bellowed. "I wish to
rule . . . as Sultan!"

The Genie was
powerless to resist.

"Genie, no!" Aladdin cried as Jafar took over the palace.

"Sorry, kid," the Genie said. "I've got a new master now."

Then Jafar made his second wish—to become a powerful sorcerer! Jafar used his evil sorcery to banish Aladdin to the snowy ends of the earth!

Luckily, Abu and the Magic Carpet were still with him.

"Now, back to Agrabah!" Aladdin cried as they sped off on the Magic Carpet.

Back at the palace, the poor Sultan was hanging from the ceiling of his throne room like a puppet. And Jafar had made Jasmine his slave!

Jafar was so busy enjoying his power that he didn't notice Aladdin sneaking into the throne room. But just as Aladdin reached for the lamp, Jafar saw his reflection in Jasmine's tiara.

"How many times do I have to kill
you, boy!" Jafar cried as he fired his snake
staff at Aladdin and trapped him.
Jasmine ran to help Aladdin, but Jafar trapped her, too.
"Princess, your time is up!" he cried.

Suddenly, Aladdin had an idea
to rid them of Jafar.

"The Genie has more power than
you'll ever have!" Aladdin told Jafar.

So, the power-hungry Jafar used
his last wish to become a genie!

But Jafar forgot one thing—all genies must live in a lamp until they are summoned by a new master. "Noooo!" Jafar cried as he was imprisoned inside a magic lamp!

As a reward for Aladdin's bravery, the Sultan changed the law so Jasmine could marry whoever she chose.

Of course, she chose Aladdin.

Aladdin used his third wish to free the
Genie. The Genie was so happy! He couldn't
wait to see the world.

Aladdin and the Genie sadly said goodbye,
but they knew they would be friends forever.